Houses Around the World

Lisa James

AF584942

Some houses keep out the cold.
Some houses keep out the heat.

Some houses even float on water!

A tent is a good house if you move a lot.

This is a yurt.
It is like a tent.
It is easy to pack away
and easy to move.

An underground house is a good house if it is very hot.

Underground houses stay cool because they are cut from rock. The walls are thick. Heat cannot get in.

A turf house is a good house if it is very cold.

Turf is made of mud and grass.
The turf walls are thick.
The cold wind cannot get in.

A floating house is a good house if you live by the water.

The house floats on the water.
It stays dry
even when the water rises.
You could get a boat to school!

A tree house is a good house if you live in the jungle.

This house is high up in the tree tops.
You would need to be good at climbing to live here!

Here are all these houses around the world.

Turf house, Iceland

Yurt, Mongolia

Tree house, Thailand

Floating house,
Cambodia
Underground house,
Australia

Which house do you like best?